BASK IN MY GLORY, YE MORTALS

"I laughed. I cried. I realized I was merely hormonal."

- AMAZON REVIEWER ON *FIFTY SHAMES GONE GREY*

"The literary equivalent of a good *Saturday Night Live* skit."

- *THE HOLLYWOOD REPORTER* ON *FIFTY SHAMES OF EARL GREY*

"I'm not even sure what happened. In that sense it was a lot like *Gone Girl*."

- AMAZON REVIEWER ON *FIFTY SHAMES GONE GREY*

ALSO BY FANNY MERKIN

Fifty Shames of Earl Grey: A Parody

FIFTY SHAMES GONE GREY

Fifty Shames Gone Grey novella previously published by 8th Circle Press as the ebook exclusive *Gone Grey: A Parody. An Earl Grey Christmas* previously published as a standalone ebook by 8th Circle Press. *Fifty Shades of Gold* originally published in *Fic: Why Fanfiction Is Taking Over the World. Writing Parody and Satire* originally published in *Shelf Pleasure.*

Cover illustrations and interior illustrations by Andrew Shaffer. Cover photograph courtesy Shutterstock.

Trade Paperback ISBN: 978-1-949769-33-3

Library Hardcover ISBN: 978-1-949769-36-4

Also available as an eBook

Published by 8th Circle Press (Louisville, KY) / Distributed by Ingram

Second Edition (First 8th Circle Press edition January 2021)

FIFTY SHAMES GONE GREY

A NOVELLA

FANNY MERKIN

INTRODUCTION BY

ANDREW SHAFFER

CONTENTS

INTRODUCTION

Since it's been almost a decade since *Fifty Shades of Grey* blew up, a refresher course is in order.

You remember the story, even if you think you've blocked it out: Anastasia Steele, a college-age virgin who has never been kissed, meets Christian Grey, the 27-year-old billionaire CEO of Grey's Enterprises Holdings. Christian is unbelievably handsome with his "tousled hair" and "expensive body wash." He is also unbelievably kinky, and he wants to share his love of BDSM (and fine wine, and classical music, and Bruce Springsteen) with Anastasia.

While Christian and Anastasia start out with "vanilla" sex acts, they gradually add spanking, bondage, riding crops, and object insertion into their repertoire. James teases the reader with an exhaustive list of sex acts and scenarios by way of a D/s contract.

"No fisting, you say. Anything else you object

to?" Christian asks Anastasia. "Anal intercourse doesn't exactly float my boat," she says. He responds, "I'll agree to [remove] the fisting, but I'd really like to claim your ass, Anastasia."

Christian even attempts to prohibit Anastasia from snacking between meals and dictate how many times a week she works out (four, if you must know). As many readers have wondered, *Is this BDSM or Weight Watchers?*

One thing that is never entirely clear is why Christian is so enamored with the heroine. "You are the most fascinating woman I know," he tells her. Why? Literally the only things the reader learns about Anastasia is that A) she prefers tea to coffee, and B) she can distinguish $3.99 body wash from $6.99 body wash by smell.

The most head-scratching scenes in *Fifty Shades of Grey,* however, involve food. Take this attempt by Anastasia to seduce Christian: "Picking up a spear of asparagus, I gaze at him and bite my lip. Then very slowly put the tip of my cold asparagus in my mouth and suck. Christian's eyes widen infinitesimally, but I notice. 'Anastasia. What are you doing?'"

Yes, honey, what the hell are you doing?

Readers ate this crap up. And why not? Was there any better indication that the US had finally limped out of the Great Recession than a zeitgeist novel featuring a CEO hero?

Christian buys Anastasia a $14,000 Thomas

Hardy first edition, an Audi A3, a MacBook, and a Blackberry. "I will buy you lots of things, Anastasia. Get used to it. I can afford it. I'm a very wealthy man," he says. He flies her around Seattle in his helicopter and offers his private jet to her.

When she protests that all of the gifts make her feel "cheap," he responds, "You're over-thinking it, Anastasia. Don't place some vague moral judgment on yourself based on what others might think. If I want to buy you a fucking car, I'll buy you a fucking car."

Who doesn't want to be pampered like that? I'll call you "Daddy" if it means a new laptop. Claim my ass, Christian! I need that 13-inch MacBook Pro with the M1 chip.

This is all a long way of saying, of course, that *Fifty Shades of Grey* holds a distinct place as one of the worst-written bestsellers of all time. (*The Da Vinci Code* fucking rocked, by the way—there was a time when bestsellers weren't absolute shit.)

In fact, you could say that *Fifty Shades* was so terrible that it was parody-proof. At one of my book events, I told the audience I would be reading from my parody *Fifty Shames of Earl Grey* (published under the pen name "Fanny Merkin"). Instead, I chose to read a selection from one of James's books... and had the crowd howling with laughter. When I revealed the ruse, the room erupted with applause.

But write a parody I did. *Fifty Shames of Earl*

Grey sold tens of thousands of copies, and became an international bestseller. It was translated into French, Czech, Italian, and Portuguese.

Once *Fifty Shades* mania died down, however, so did the publishing world's appetite for a *Fifty Shames* sequel. No matter. Eventually, I wrote and self-published a novella (*Fifty Shames Gone Grey*, a parody of *Gone Girl*) and a tie-in short story ("An Earl Grey Christmas," also included in this newly expanded edition of the novella).

Is the book you hold in your hands the final chapter of the Earl Grey saga? Perhaps. But that's why I've loaded it a plethora of bonus material, from essays to unused (but hilarious) promotional artwork. If you're gonna go out, why not go out with a bang (pun intended)?

— Andrew Shaffer
(a.k.a. Fanny Merkin)
Louisville, KY
January 2021

FIFTY SHAMES GONE GREY

A NOVELLA

FANNY MERKIN

Earl Grey's wife disappears on their fifth wedding anniversary. He quickly becomes the prime suspect, leaving him with no friends except for his twin sister, Goonie. Can movie star Tyler Perry help him find his wife...or is she just gone, girl?

Apologies to Gillian Flynn

CHAPTER 1

When I think of my wife, I think about her head.

No, not the head she gives me while I'm flying my helicopter. I'm talking about the head on her neck, the one with the eyes and nose and ears and all that other stuff.

Before she wakes up most mornings, I lie beside her staring at the back of her head. What's inside, I wonder? If I took a power-saw to her skull, would I find a brain in there? Or is her head filled with straw, like the Scarecrow from *The Wizard of Oz*?

It's not as crazy a question as it sounds. My wife is not the sharpest knife in the drawer.

At first, I attributed this to her public schooling. She was twenty-one when we met, a virgin in more than one sense of the word. She thought BDSM was some "Zumba thing." She'd never had an e-mail address in her life—because she thought they were "too expensive." Even odder, she had no clue who Tom Cruise was. I mean, really? Even starving children in third-world countries know who Tom Cruise is. Some of them probably worship him as a god, like I do.

These were the thoughts occupying me the morning of our fifth wedding anniversary as I ran a hand through her silky brown hair. *What are you thinking, Anna?* I wondered, picking out the gum. *Is there anyone at home in there?*

Don't get me wrong: I love my wife. That's never been in question. I'll continue loving her, even if there's a hamster on a wheel inside her skull.

Anna let out a loud, wet belch. She's always burping or passing gas in her sleep. Oh, the money you could make if you could harness the air that comes out of her for energy!

Alas, we weren't in such a pickle that we needed to go that far for money. But things weren't great. At least we had a roof over our heads. We lived in a trailer on her parents' property on the outskirts of Portland, Oregon. Neither of us was happy about the arrangement.

"Well, fuck me gently with a chainsaw," she'd said the day we moved in.

I hoped she was speaking metaphorically, because that was a little too kinky even for me. It was obvious she was plenty angry, but what could we do?

Don't blame me, Anna. Blame the economy, blame bad luck, blame it on the rain.

Once upon a time, I'd been a successful businessman. By the age of twenty-seven, I was CEO of my own company, the humbly named Earl Grey Corporation. I had my own building in downtown Seattle—a 175-story steel erection. I had a helicopter, a yacht, and a Duck Dynasty-branded camouflage Segway. I could explain the nature of my work, but it would make for a dry book. If you want an idea of how the financial world operates, I suggest watching *The Wolf of Wall Street.*

After ten years, a series of bad investments ended my wild ride overnight. Who knew the market for kale would dry up so quickly after people figured out it was just wilted lettuce?

Three weeks after my company folded, Anna lost her job at Amazon. The bald man laid her off and that was it. We were just two jobless twentysomethings, adrift in Seattle. Things had gotten so bad that I finally understood the appeal of grunge music.

We spent weeks on the couch of our mansion catching up on our Netflix queue. *Orange Is the New Black. Sharknado 2: The Second One. Gilmore Girls.* When the power company cut our electricity, we switched to streaming Netflix on our iPhones. Eventually, our iPhones were cut off too. We huddled together in the darkness, shivering and wondering if we'd ever make it to the *Gilmore Girls* series finale.

"My mother and stepfather have Netflix," Anna said.

I scoffed at her suggestion. "They're nudists. Even worse, they live in that podunk city to the south, Portland."

"It's not like you haven't seen them naked before," she said. "And they won't even be home. They're at their winter place in Florida."

"Fine, fine," I said. We both knew we were on the road to ruin. What we needed was a distraction. We never expected the vacation would be permanent.

When we returned home after a week in Portland on her parents' plastic-covered couch, there was a padlock on our front door. The bank had foreclosed on our house. That's when we heard our car start up. We turned around just in time to see a banker driving away with it.

We hustled to our backyard helipad. The helicopter was untouched...for now. I opened the door for Anna.

She hesitated. "Last time you flew this thing, you ran into the Space Needle. All of those people died. *You* almost died."

"I can assure you I'm not going to hit the Space Needle again," I said. "You can trust me. Just get in. Time's a-wasting."

She climbed in. I hit a bunch of buttons just like I'd seen my flight instructor do a million times. Before I knew it, we were soaring in the air, over Puget Sound...and right into the Space Needle.

This time, only a dozen people lost their lives. All tourists, so big whoop.

Using the last of our petty cash, we bought a mobile home and parked it behind her parents' house. They had a spare bedroom, but I couldn't fathom waking up every morning and seeing her stepfather's naked rear end. Her mother's, maybe—her mother wasn't bad-looking for her age. I had what was left of the helicopter towed to Portland as well. *She might not ever fly again*, I thought, *but I couldn't just abandon her*.

Anna had a fit when she saw the tow truck in the driveway. "You love that damned helicopter so much, you should have married it!" Anna shouted, storming away.

Don't be absurd, I thought. *You can't marry a helicopter in this country—yet.*

We expected to get back on our feet in no time.

Two years later, we were still broke.

Anna rolled lazily onto her back. I hid the power-saw on the floor before she opened her eyes. There had to be an easier way to find out what was in her head than sawing the top of her skull off. Maybe a laser?

"What time is it?" she asked me.

"I haven't the slightest idea," I said. "It doesn't really matter, does it? We don't have anywhere to be."

"*I* don't have anywhere to be," she said. "*You* have a job interview today."

"A job—" I began, then stopped. Oh, yeah. A "job interview." Of course. How could I have forgotten. I glanced at the alarm clock on the nightstand. Nine-thirty.

"Guess I'd better be on my way," I said, swinging my legs out of bed.

I could feel Anna's eyes on me as I dressed. I examined myself in the full-length mirror. It had been forever since I'd worn my dark gray suit.

"Hold on," Anna said, disappearing into the closet. She emerged with one of my bold ties, the one I'd been wearing the day we met. She wrapped it around my neck and fixed it up.

"There," she said, standing back. "Better."

I stared at myself in the mirror again. If I saw me on the street, would I still mistake me for the richest man on the planet? The smiley-faces on the tie leered back at me, mocking me. It was time to go.

CHAPTER 2

I entered the chocolate bar. Darkness enveloped me. When my eyes finally adjusted to the dim lighting, I could see that there was only one other person drinking in Chocoteria: a sad clown. I saw him every time I was there. When I first noticed him, I thought to myself, *Look at that chocoholic*. Later on, I began to realize he probably had the same thought about me. If, that is, clowns are sentient beings capable of thought.

My twin sister was working behind the bar. I was still getting used to the idea of having a sister. Until a few years ago, I'd believed I was an only child, orphaned after my mother died in a horrific accident. Turns out my mother faked her own death to escape the loan sharks on her ass. When she returned from the dead and back into my life, she revealed I had a twin sister she'd lost in a poker game when we were babies—the same way she'd once lost me.

I used my vast wealth and resources to track my sister down. We weren't identical twins–thank Christ. I wouldn't call her unattractive, but she looks like Sloth from *The Goonies* in a sloppy black wig. That's where her nickname comes from.

"How's it hanging, Goonie?" I said, sliding onto a barstool.

Goonie poured me a pint of Hershey's syrup. "You're all dressed up."

"I was supposed to have a job interview at Walmart," I said. "It was cancelled yesterday. They said I was overqualified. Not surprising, since I was so rich at one point that I owned Walmart."

"Listen up, brother: I love you, but you're overqualified for *every* job. You're the most attractive, amazing, attractive, intelligent, attractive man I know."

I threw my hands up. "Exactly! That's what I've been trying to tell Anna. She just doesn't get it."

"She thinks you're at the interview, doesn't she?"

I sipped my Hershey's and nodded. "It's our five-year anniversary."

"Congratulations," Goonie said. "My longest relationship lasted five weeks."

"That's not surprising," I muttered.

"Keep your head up. Things will turn around–they have to. Is Anna going to do one of her, what are they called?"

"Treasure hunts."

When we first met, I was the one who liked to play games—erotic roleplaying games, like BDSM (Bards, Dragons, Sorcery, and Magick). It took some convincing to bring Anna into my world. Soon, however, she became the one initiating games—both in and out of the bedroom. On our first anniversary, to show me how far she'd come, Anna created a treasure hunt.

The hunter had become the hunted.

She left a series of clues, each one leading to the next, until finally reaching the end: A private concert in our garage by my favorite band, Nickelback. So that's why their tour bus had been parked outside all day while I followed her clues around the house.

Every year, the treasure hunt grew in scope, until last year's went a full week. Even though we didn't have much money for gifts, the clues led straight to the greatest gift a guy could ever ask for. This time, I *am* talking about her head in a helicopter.

"I figure I'll have a few pints, then go home and see what she's cooked up this year," I told my sister. I left off the part about the blowjob—though if last year's treasure hunt was any indication, Anna's "gift" could be a week or two away. Holy blue balls, Batman.

The phone rang. Goonie picked it up, listened for a moment, and rolled her eyes. "You're in luck," she said to the caller. "He's right here."

I took the phone from her. "This is Earl."

"It's Maureen," the woman said. Anna's mother. Ugh. "I thought you should know that your door is wide open, and that pet rock of yours is outside. I don't know where Anna is, since neither of you can afford cell phones, but I figured you'd be at your sister's chocolate bar. Some catch you turned out to be, huh?"

I sighed. Anna knew she wasn't supposed to let Littler Sebastian out.

"I'll be home to check on him," I said.

CHAPTER 3

I pulled our car up the gravel driveway, past Anna's parents' house and to our little trailer. The car was a loaner her father had given us until we could get on our own feet and buy a car of our own. I hated taking it out. Who wants to be seen driving around in a 1970 Gremlin? It's the ugly Christmas sweater of automobiles. You didn't even need to turn it off—just roll it to a stop and wait for it to stall.

Littler Sebastian was sitting on the steps. The damn rock wasn't smart enough to go any farther than that. The front door was wide open, just as Anna's mother had said. Maybe Anna was airing the trailer out after cutting the cheese.

Maureen was standing out on her back porch, naked as the day she was born, waiting for me to do something. I waved at her to let her know, *Hey, I got this, I'm not the good-for-nothing sitcom husband you think I am.* Instead of returning my salutation, she extended a middle finger and took a drag off her Virginia Slim. In-laws, amirite?

I picked Littler Sebastian up. He weighed almost four pounds the last time we'd taken him in to the vet. "Let's go find Mommy," I told him, cradling him in my hand like a baseball.

I stepped inside.

The living room was trashed. Junk everywhere. It looked like burglars had ransacked our place. Of course, this was typical of our trailer. Neither one of us was gifted in the art of cleanliness.

"Anna, you home?"

No answer.

I checked out our bedroom. No Anna. The ironing board was out, and the iron was still on. Someone had been here; Anna had never ironed anything in her life.

I returned to the living room and went to set Littler Sebastian down on the coffee table...and realized that I couldn't, because the table was in pieces on the floor. Glass everywhere. There'd been a struggle, I was sure of it. Someone had come into our home and started using our iron, and then they'd fought with my wife—and one of them had gone through the coffee table.

I rushed to the kitchen.

Empty.

That's when the refrigerator caught my eye.

What ran through my mind was too horrible to

contemplate. Had my wife been chopped up and stuffed inside the fridge like in some awful comic book from the nineties? Slowly, I opened the refrigerator door and peeked inside through half-closed eyes...and cried out in horror.

I slammed the door and fell to the ground, crying and shaking.

The milk was six days past its expiration date.

Anna might not have been in the fridge, but that was little consolation. Something had happened, something bad. A kidnapping, possibly a murder—the signs were all there. There would be no treasure hunt, no BJ at the end of this rainbow.

Anna Grey was gone, girl.

CHAPTER 4

I watched the cops ride their unicycles up the driveway from the front window. They stopped to stare at my naked mother-in-law, who was smoking another cigarette on her back porch. Why couldn't she have gone missing, and not her daughter?

I opened the front door and met them on the steps. The officers—one man, one woman—both had thick hipster beards. They were wearing vintage uniforms and bowler hats. A patch on the man's sleeve read "Portland PD: Gluten-Free Since 1998."

"Mr. Grey?" the woman said. "I'm Officer Flynn. This is Officer Fincher. You reported a break-in?"

I waved for them to follow me inside. Flynn paused while passing me to sniff the air. "Have you been drinking chocolate, Mr. Grey?"

"What?" I said. My voice was small and incredulous, like a man who'd just been caught by his wife in bed with another woman.

"You have a chocolate milk mustache," the officer said. "You might want to clean that off."

I wiped my face with my palm, and we went inside. The cops scanned the destruction in the living room.

"Did you notice anything missing?" Flynn asked.

"My wife," I said. Unfortunately, it came out sounding like Borat: *my wiiiiiife.* "I would call her, but she doesn't have a phone. And neither do I."

Fincher narrowed his eyes at me. "Not even a prepaid cell?"

I shook my head. "We had her micro-chipped, but the GPS doesn't work if you stop paying the monthly fee."

"Sounds about right," Flynn said. "Mind if we take a look around?"

"Be my guest."

They poked their snouts around the living room, the kitchen, the bedroom. I followed them.

"How long have you lived here?" Flynn asked.

"Two years," I said. "We moved from Seattle."

The officers exchanged a weary look. I knew the look well. Portlanders were suspicious of people from Seattle. The bigger city's cosmopolitan vibe was at odds with the small-town, eat local, shit local ethos of Portland.

"You two have any children?" Flynn asked.

I shook my head. "Not anymore. We had a son, Chris—but he was repossessed by the bank."

Fincher nodded knowingly. “Lot of folks having financial trouble these days.”

We returned to the living room. “Is there something you can do?” I asked. “Like, put out a bulletin for her?”

“I suppose,” Flynn began. “We just, ah, haven’t ever worked a missing persons case. I’m not sure what the protocol is. This isn’t Seattle, you know.”

Fincher adjusted his belt. “It’s kind of exciting, isn’t it? I mean, not for *you*,” he said, nodding toward me.

“There must be something you can do,” I pleaded.

Flynn rubbed her scruffy chin. “You know what, there is. We just got a fingerprint kit down at the station. I suppose I could radio back and have someone bring it out. We could dust for fingerprints.”

“Like on a TV show!” Fincher exclaimed, clapping and jumping up and down.

“Hey, is that...” Fincher’s voice trailed off. I followed his eyes across the room to the DVDs we’d borrowed from her parents. He picked up a case and began reading the back. “Yeah, it is. Have you seen this one, Flynn?”

I peered over her shoulder at the DVD they were looking at. *Dexter* season four.

“Yeah,” she said. “This is the one where his wife—”

“Seriously?” I said, snatching it out of Fincher’s

hands. "I'm only halfway through. No spoilers, please."

Fincher seriously grew very serious. "There's no need to get an attitude with us. We're here to help you. That's, like, the Portland police department motto: TO HELP PEOPLE AND STUFF."

"I thought your motto was TO PROTECT AND TO SERVE," I said.

They exchanged skeptical glances. "If you don't want our help, then we can just leave," Flynn said. "I'm sure there's a bird caught in a tree that needs our help."

If this was Portland's finest, they weren't going to be much help finding my missing wife. I buried my head in my hands.

"You okay there, Mr. Grey?" Flynn asked.

I stared at her. "My wife is missing. I'm pretty far from okay."

"You know who's responsible in like ninety-nine percent of cases?" Flynn asked.

I shrugged. "I don't know. Who?"

She looked irritated with me. "I don't know either. That's why I was asking you."

"Hey, wait a minute," Fincher said, picking a book up from amidst the shattered remains of the coffee table. "What's this?"

One glance at its pink floral cover, and I knew immediately what it was. I don't know how I'd been so oblivious as to overlook it until now. "It's my wife's diary."

Flynn scrunched her face up. "What is this, the year eighteen-hundred? I thought everyone spilled their guts online these days. What kind of person would keep a private journal?"

"It sounds suspicious," Fincher said, flipping through the pages.

"She doesn't usually just leave it out like that," I said. "She keeps it hidden. I've asked her before what she puts in there, but, you know how women are."

Fincher glared at me. "No, I don't know. Why don't you tell me all about women, Mr. Grey?"

"Oh, uh," I scrambled. "They're always, uh, you know. Doing things. Secret things."

Flynn nodded. "I know what you're saying. My wife's the same way. Always doing things."

I breathed a sigh of relief. At least someone understood me.

"I growl with frustration," Fincher said.

"Excuse me?"

"It's the first line of your wife's diary," the officer said, holding up the book. *"I growl with frustration."*

CHAPTER 5

I growl with frustration at my reflection in the mirror. My hair is fifty shades of messed up. Why is it so kinky and out of control? I need to stop sleeping with it wet. As I brush my long brown hair, the girl in the mirror with brown eyes too big for her head stares back at me. Wait...my eyes are blue! It dawns on me that I haven't been looking into the mirror—I've been staring at a poster of Kristen Stewart for five minutes. My own hair is fine.

The situation I'm in, however, is still fifty shades of messed up. My roommate, Kathleen, has the brown bottle flu. What a B. She was supposed to be the one interviewing this mega-corporate beefcake for Boardroom Hotties *magazine. Since she's too busy throwing up buckets of puke into the toilet, I've been volunteered to do her dirty work. (The interview, not cleaning up her vomit.) I am mere weeks away from graduating from college with a liberal arts bachelor's degree. Instead of studying for my final exams, though, I'm about to ride my bike three and a half hours from Portland, Oregon, to downtown Seattle to meet with Earl Grey, the fabulously wealthy CEO of the Earl Grey Corporation.*

I sank into the couch as Officer Fincher read aloud from Anna's diary as if it were a steamy romance novel. I remembered the day Anna was describing quite well—it was the day we met. No wonder she'd never let me read her diary before. It was a sprawling hot mess. I don't know how Anna ever expected to "make it" in the publishing industry in any capacity, seeing as how she could barely string together a decent sentence.

Officer Fincher got to the part where Anna first laid eyes on me:

> *I open my eyes and stare down at Mr. Grey and HOLY MOTHER EFFING SPARKLY VAMPIRES IS HE HOT.*

I stifled a laugh, because that was the same thing going through my mind when Anna cartwheeled into my office: *HOLY MOTHER EFFING SPARKLY VAMPIRES AM I HOT.*

Fincher skipped a few pages and read another entry. This time, it wasn't so flattering:

> *I open my bedroom door...and find the handsomest man in the whole world, Earl Grey, sitting on my bed!*
>
> *"What are you doing here?" I say. What a creeper!*
>
> *"I could ask you the same thing," he says.*
>
> *"I live here," I say.*
>
> *"I bought the duplex from Kathleen's parents this afternoon," he says. "I'm your landlord now. So technically I live here too."*

The way Anna wrote about our courtship made it sound like I was a filthy rich, mentally unbalanced sociopath who stalked her until she gave in. Maybe there was some truth to that. It's true that I threw my money around without abandon. It's also true that I crossed many ethical lines in my pursuit of Anna Steal. But wasn't it all worth it, in the end? I'd known from the moment we met that we were destined to be. Cupid had been on my side. I knew that, because I'd paid him off.

Fincher flipped ahead in the diary, this time landing on a page that made his eyeballs nearly pop out of their sockets. "You guys were into some kinky stuff," he said, quickly flipping the pages again. If Anna had recorded even half of the kinky things we did together, then Fincher would need to take the world's longest bath when he got home to feel clean again.

"Here's the last entry, dated two days ago," Fincher said.

> *I feel so alive! It's a beautiful day out, and the birds are singing.*
>
> *Oh, wait. Those aren't birds—it's just the radio alarm clock. I was wondering how the birds learned Adele.*
>
> *Anyway, I roll over and Earl is gone. He's been waking up earlier and earlier lately, going God knows where. He says he's picking up job applications and interviewing. Half the time I believe him...the other half, not so much. He doesn't even dress up when he goes out! I suspect he's been hanging out at that chocolate bar with his sister.*
>
> *But this morning, I'm not worried about where my husband is. I'm more concerned with my morning sickness.*
>
> *I shoot out of bed, and barely make it to the bathroom before throwing up. As my eyes tear up, I pull my birth control pills out of the medicine cabinet. Three left... I try to do the math in my head, but I'm no good with numbers. Have I missed a couple of days? Have I missed a couple of months?*

One visit to the pharmacy later, I'm back in the bathroom trying to decipher the results of a pregnancy test. Slowly, the blue letters materialize on the end of the stick.

K-N-O-C-K-E-D U-P.

Oh no.

What will Earl do when he finds out I'm pregnant again? He's been acting strange lately. It must be all the chocolate. Will he ask me to terminate the pregnancy? And if I say no, will he try to end my life?

I hope I'm wrong. But I worry, still. Sometimes he looks at me like...like he's thinking about doing harm to me. I can see it in his eyes, and I think: My husband might kill me.

So if you find this diary and I'm dead, do the math.

Because I can't do the math.

Math is hard.

CHAPTER 6

After reading the final diary entry, Flynn and Fincher asked me to come down to the police station with them for a formal interview. They said they'd seen police interview suspects on *NCIS: Park Slope* before.

Fincher opened the door to their interrogation room and flipped the light on. "Have a seat," he said, gesturing to the chairs on opposite sides of a ping-pong table.

"Are you sure this is the interrogation room?" I asked, sitting down.

Fincher seated himself across the net from me and looked around. There was an exercise bike in one corner, and a stack of board games in another.

"Like I said, we don't do too many interrogations around here," Fincher said.

Flynn closed the door. "We're just going to have a friendly chat. We want to make sure our bases are covered, in case the FBI comes knocking on our door. First thing, we need to get a DNA sample from you."

I stood and began unzipping my pants.

"From the inside of your cheek," Flynn said, opening a plastic bag.

"Oh," I said. "Of course."

She swabbed inside my cheek and sealed the sample.

"So how long have you been living here in Portland?" Fincher asked.

"A couple of years," I said. "Two."

"And where is your wife from, originally?"

"Her mother's womb," I said. "If you want to go back further, you could check with her father's testicles."

"We may do that," Flynn said, writing a note down.

"Does your wife have any drug or alcohol problems?" her partner asked.

I tried hard to think about this question. Did Anna have any issues with substance abuse? She'd done a little ecstasy and cocaine in college—and turned tricks to feed the monkey on her back—but then again who hasn't? If those are "drugs," then I guess you could call her a "drug addict."

I shrugged. "Nothing out of the ordinary."

Fincher pushed the diary across the table toward me. "You know the final entry in here points a finger at you. Why did you hide your wife's pregnancy from us?"

"I didn't tell you about it because I didn't know," I said.

Yes, I told them, I'd found the empty pregnancy test box in the trash. Yes, I'd found the positive pregnancy test in the trash. And, yes, Anna had off-handedly said, "Earl, I'm pregnant."

But how was I supposed to put all these clues together? I wasn't a detective.

"This is all very interesting," Flynn said, scribbling more notes in her notebook.

I craned my neck forward, and got a glimpse of what she was writing just before she angled the notebook away from me. *Earl Grey. Greek Yogurt.*

"Are you making a grocery list?" I asked, throwing my hands up in disbelief. My wife was missing, and the police weren't even listening to me!

Flynn frowned. "This isn't a grocery list. I'm writing down a list of suspects."

"Greek Yogurt isn't the name of a person," I protested.

"It's a gangster nickname," Flynn said. "Like in the *Dick Tracy* comics. It's just like that."

"It's the stupidest gangster nickname I've ever heard," I muttered. Her obvious lie irritated me to no end. Flynn and Fincher weren't doing a good cop/bad cop routine; they were doing an incompetent cop/incompetent cop routine. "Are we done here?"

They let me go, with the instructions to keep in touch if I heard from my wife. On my way out of the police station, I passed a hardened criminal in handcuffs being fingerprinted. He had jet-black hair and tanned, chiseled features. Three white teardrops were tattooed on either side of his eyes. My attention, however, zeroed in on the gothic script tattoo on his neck. There were just two words, but they sucker-punched me right in the wedding tackle: GREEK YOGURT.

Officer Flynn hadn't been lying. She'd been compiling a list of suspects after all...and I was at the top of her list.

CHAPTER 7

That night, the all-points-bulletin went out: Anna Grey, wife of the infamous Earl Grey (who was not an English earl, and who did not like tea—in fact he couldn't stand the stuff, the wordy bulletin read), was missing.

Anna's mother and stepfather organized a press conference at a local high school gymnasium the next morning. We rode together in my car, not saying a word to each other. They probably suspected I had something to do with her disappearance, but didn't come right out and say it. I felt like half the world thought I had something to do with her disappearance. I'd read the *Oregonian*'s write-up, and the comments below it weren't flattering. Then again, have you ever read a positive comment on the Internet?

By the time we arrived at eleven-thirty, the

gymnasium was packed—mostly with students playing basketball.

"What's going on here?" I asked Anna's mother, who hadn't even bothered to dress for the occasion. They didn't own any clothing, but still.

"Looks like they're playing basketball," Maureen said.

"I know that. I thought you reserved the gym?"

She shrugged. "I didn't reserve anything. I just thought it sounded like a big place, like where you'd hold a press conference."

A handful of reporters were standing around, waiting for the event to begin. There were a dozen or so men and women in the stands, either there for us or for the kids playing basketball. Goonie waved to me from across the gym, and hustled over to meet me.

"How are you holding up, brother?" she asked, kissing me on the lips and eagerly grabbing my butt.

Maureen shot us a look of disapproval. "Here we go with the twin-cest..."

"I wish our mother were here," Goonie said, ignoring my mother-in-law.

I nodded. Our mother had spontaneously combusted a year earlier. Goonie walked into her room at the assisted living facility one day to find a pile of ashes on her bed. What a gruesome way to go. At least we'd saved money on her cremation.

"You don't think Anna could have...gone the

same way, do you?" Goonie asked. "Spontaneous combustion runs in families."

"Not in this case," I said. "Anna and our mother weren't blood relatives. Blood relatives don't get married, you know."

"That's a shame," Goonie said.

"Please, a woman is missing."

"Someone's grumpy today," she said, twisting my nipples through my shirt.

"I feel terrible." I sighed. "Didn't sleep at all last night."

"Up all night worrying about your wife?"

I shook my head. "Playing *Grand Theft Auto*."

A woman I recognized from our church put a hand on my shoulder. Natalie. I vaguely recalled she was friends with Anna. She'd volunteered to serve as an adhoc PR director for our little conference.

"It's time. They're going to want to hear a word from her husband," Natalie said.

We made our way to the front of the bleachers, where she'd set up an easel with a three-foot tall drawing of Anna's face. "I could have found an actual photo," I whispered to her.

"My daughter wanted to help out with the search effort," Natalie explained. "I thought you'd be grateful."

I forced a smile. The last thing I needed was one of the few people on my side to turn against me. "It's great. Tell her thank you," I said, staring at the crude drawing. It was nothing more than a circle with two dots for eyes and a crooked smile. The hair was scribbled on.

Cameras flashed around us. I hadn't even been aware cameras still existed outside of cellphones, but apparently reporters had been hoarding them.

Anna's stepfather addressed the small crowd from behind a podium, which thankfully hid his twig and berries. "Our daughter, Anna, is a wonderful girl. Our only child. I could tell you about how smart and beautiful she is, but I'm not going to lie. She's dumber than Harry and Lloyd after double lobotomies. But I will say this: she's such a kind, sweet girl. And she's not half-bad on the eyes." Maureen slapped his arm.

"We want her back," he continued. "Whoever did this—" (and here he glared at me) "—we want her back. Please."

When I took the microphone next, I sensed the crowd beginning to turn against me. So I tried to open with a little levity. I tapped the microphone. "Mic check, mic check. One, one, two, two, three, three...*too many rappers, still not enough emcees...*"

The crowd stared at me with befuddled looks.

"Guess there's not a lot of Beastie fans out there," I said. "Well, anyway, I'm not here to rap. My name is Earl Grey, and I'm here to talk to you about my wife. She went missing—"

A basketball struck me in the back of the head. I

shook off the cobwebs and picked up my speech. "As I was saying, my wife went missing—"

WHAP.

Another basketball hit me, this time in the side of the face. I scooped it up and spun around. Twelve eighth-grade boys were standing there with their arms crossed. "Which one of you keeps losing control of his balls?" I yelled.

"What's it to you, old man?" a pizza-faced little Wesley Crusher asked.

"What did you just call me?"

"Old man," the prick said, a little louder. "Maybe you need to turn your hearing aid up."

I dribbled the basketball, advancing toward the pack of mongrels. In the heat of the moment, I'd completely forgotten about the audience waiting for me to finish my speech. When I was three feet from the kids, I passed the ball to the one who'd been mouthing off to me. "One on one, me and you," I said, untucking my shirt.

"You're on, Grandpa," the kid said, dribbling the basketball.

I kicked his ass, of course.

That doesn't mean I didn't lose. I lost big time—on social media. You've probably seen the photo of me dunking the ball with my missing wife's picture in the background. Within minutes of the AP photographer snapping it, the photo spread around the Internet like an STD in a nursing home.

I left the gym without Anna's parents. They said they didn't want to ride anywhere with their daughter's murderer, and would take their chances being killed by an Uber driver instead.

Going back home or to my sister's bar were both out of the question. Wherever I went, the reporters were bound to be thick as maggots on a corpse. Instead, I just put my foot to the gas pedal and drove with no destination in mind.

I careened around Portland until my gas tank was empty, and then drove some more. Finally, the car shuddered and died in an unfamiliar neighborhood. I stumbled out and looked around. My eyes landed on a bright pink building. The last thing I remember was reading the sign on the door as I entered: Voodoo Doughnuts. Then everything went black.

CHAPTER 8

"Rise and shine, Homer Simpson."

Although my eyes were closed, I rejoiced at the sound of Anna's voice. It felt like I was coming out of a long slumber.

"I just had the worst dream," I mumbled, slowly opening my eyes. As soon as they'd adjusted to the light, I realized I hadn't been dreaming—or maybe I was still dreaming. A well-dressed gentleman was crouched over me. Anna was nowhere to be found.

"Oh, really? You can tell me all about it once we get you cleaned up," the man said.

"I...I know you," I said. "You're Tyler Perry, the actor."

He smiled. "The one and only." He paused, looking me up and down. "Jesus, though—look at yourself. You're a mess, my man."

I was sitting up against a concrete wall outdoors, my shirt covered in sprinkles and donut crumbs. I looked down at my hands and saw they were stained with a rainbow of colors, as if I'd just jacked off a unicorn.

"I've seen better days," I said, rising to my feet and dusting myself off.

"Let's get some coffee in you," he said. "Not here, though."

I looked uneasily back at the donut shop entrance. "What...what happened to me?"

"You don't remember? You ordered two-dozen donuts—which they served to you in a small wooden casket. You kept stuffing yourself with them, apparently, and went carb crazy. After finishing the casket, you jumped the counter and started eating everything in sight: donuts, coffee cups, a couple of bucks in change. An employee tazed you, but you kept shoveling things in your mouth until you passed out."

"They didn't call the cops."

Tyler Perry shook his head. "I was standing in line, watching the whole thing go down. I recognized you. Earl Grey, the ex-billionaire. The man who financed my first three films. I told them I'd take care of you, and dragged you out here. I've been waiting for you to wake up for a couple of hours."

I didn't remember financing his movies, but that doesn't mean it didn't happen—when you're on top of the world, you have your fingers in so many pies you can't keep them straight. And nobody has longer fingers than Earl Grey.

We found a Starbucks down the street and took a seat by the window. I explained my predicament to him over coffee. I was never a fan of Starbucks–it tastes like burnt ass, after all—but was thankful for a sympathetic ear. "So what do you think?" I asked Tyler Perry.

"Are you asking if I think you killed her?"

"Killed her, kidnapped her, whatever. Everyone seems to think I had something to do with her disappearance."

"I just have one question for you, and I want you to answer it honestly: Do you love her?"

What an absurd question, I thought. I'd never heard anything so offensive in my life. "Of course I love my wife," I said. "I wouldn't have married her otherwise."

Tyler Perry shrugged. "A lot can change in five years. A man's heart can change."

"I love her, and I'm not going to stop loving her—even if she turns out to be alive and this whole 'disappearance' has been nothing more than a treasure hunt gone wrong."

Tyler Perry set his coffee down. He stared deeply into my eyes with a soulful gaze. "What would you say if I told you it *was* a treasure hunt gone wrong? That your wife is alive and well, and loves you very much? That she didn't think this through all the way? That all she meant to do was play a little game of hide and seek, and forgot to leave clues because she doesn't always use her brain?"

"I would say...that sounds a lot like my wife. But how could you know that?"

"What if I also told you that *I'm your wife?"*

My jaw dropped to the floor. Tyler Perry picked it up and handed it back to me.

"Impossible," I said, snapping my jaw back on.

"Nothing's impossible," he said.

"This is impossible," I countered, pointing a finger at his chest. "You expect me to believe that I've been married to MTV Movie Award-winning actor, director, screenwriter, playwright, and producer Tyler Perry for the past five years? And that I didn't notice?"

He nodded.

"But Anna's mother and stepfather..."

"Actors," he said. "With no wardrobe budget."

I shook my head. "Why should I believe you?"

He stared at me with brown eyes that seemed to know no depths. They pulled me in, like two *Star Trek* tractor beams. "You should believe me," he said, "because I love you. Love makes the impossible possible."

Tyler Perry held out a hand to me. Could what he was saying be true? Anna and I had laughed at his Madea movies many a night. How had I never noticed that the man on screen portraying the elderly woman was the very same person next to me on the couch? Compounding the strangeness was the fact that Anna was a twentysomething white girl, while Tyler Perry was a middle-aged black man. These are the kind of things that generally don't escape my notice. Of course, when we first hooked up I'd been distracted with work. And during our five years of marriage, I'd been too preoccupied with my crumbling finances and our relocation to really be present with my wife. If only I'd paid attention to her, I would have known the truth earlier!

"What do you say?" Tyler Perry asked. "Will you forgive me for being so silly?"

I took his hand in mine. It felt warm and familiar. "I've loved you since the day you walked into my office, Anna. Er, Tyler. The fact that you're not the person you said you were...well, that doesn't matter. We all make mistakes. All that matters is who you are on the inside. And inside, I can see you're still the one I love."

With that, I pulled Tyler Perry close to me and pressed my lips against his. We kissed deeply and passionately, the kind of kiss that could break the Internet. I put my body weight into the kiss, really pressing into him. Something hard and uncompromising pressed back into my thigh. *Can't believe I never noticed* that...

Tyler Perry saw the surprised look on my face and broke away from me. He reached into his pocket and pulled out Littler Sebastian. "So where do we go from here?" he asked me, petting our pet rock.

"Where do we go?" I repeated, smiling wide. For the first time in a long time, I was happy. Although my wife's game of hide and seek had gone terribly awry, it had made me realize just how much I loved her—and how much I'd taken her for granted. Or him. Whatever. We'd figure out the pronouns later. "We go home. Back to Seattle."

He looked glum. "I want to move out of that trailer, too. Unfortunately, love doesn't pay the bills—and neither do my movies. Do you know anyone who watches them?"

"No," I said. "But I'm going back into finance. I read about a seventeen-year-old the other day who made seventy-two million dollars trading penny stocks. If he can do it, so can I."

"That story was a hoax."

"Then I'll do what I did before: sell my plasma."

"You made your fortune selling your blood?" he asked. "How much did you sell, exactly?"

"A lot," I said gravely. "That's the reason I was as pale as a vampire when we met."

"I thought you *were* a vampire, on more than one occasion. You used to wear those fangs..."

I shrugged. "We could spend all day trying to explain the past. Or we could just start over. A ret-con. You and me. We may be broke, but we've got each other. Somehow, some way, we're going to get back on top of the world and screw its brains out."

We fistbumped. "I was going to save this for later, but I did get you another surprise for our anniversary," Tyler Perry said. "I fixed up your helicopter. It's parked behind Voodoo Doughnuts. Just...just be careful with it this time."

"Of course," I said. "When have I ever done anything reckless?"

You're not going to believe what happened next.

Okay, maybe you will.

When I'm finally moved out of this intensive care unit—and Tyler Perry wakes up from his medically-induced coma—I'm going to petition the city of Seattle to move that damn Space Needle.

AN EARL GREY CHRISTMAS

A SHORT STORY IN SIX PARTS

FANNY MERKIN

In this short story taking place prior to the events of Fifty Shames Gone Grey, *Anna searches a Seattle warehouse for the perfect holiday gift for her husband. What do you get the man who has everything? A BJ, of course. (That's* basketball jersey, *you pervs.)*

AUTHOR'S NOTE

Some readers may be thrown by the fact that, although this story is narrated by Anna, she never mentions her true identity (as revealed in *Fifty Shames Gone Grey*). It's not a continuity error! Similar to the novel *Fifty Shames of Earl Grey*, "An Earl Grey Christmas" is transcribed from Anna's diary—which, as we saw in *Fifty Shames Gone Grey*, was written with the knowledge that Earl Grey would read it. Again: it's *not* a continuity error. You fucking nerds.

CHAPTER 1

It was Christmas Eve, and I was working. This was nothing new, of course, as I worked in one of Amazon's massive shipping warehouses and the holiday season meant plenty of overtime. It was a little like being an elf in Santa's workshop, if Santa was a bald geek and elves were a couple of feet taller and a couple of degrees sadder. Not that I needed the money: I was married to Earl Grey, a man so rich he once bought every seat in a movie theater just so we could watch *The Avengers* without having to smell fanboys wetting their pants. However, I think of myself as an independent woman. I wasn't going to give up my job just because I had tons of money, and my job sucked donkey balls.

Not that everything was going as planned. I had hoped to work my way up to an editorial position within Amazon's publishing division, but after two years was still stuck in the warehouse. My husband, who was the majority shareholder in the company, wanted to put in a good word for me, but I would hear none of it. If I was going to make it in the publishing industry, I was going to do it on my own terms.

"Anna!" my supervisor yelled. I looked around, but I was the only Anna in the warehouse. Also, my supervisor was looking directly at me. She often did that when she was talking to people.

I set the box of ebooks I was carrying back on the shelf. "Yes," I said. "What can I do for you?"

"There's a call for you," she said, handing me her cell phone.

I pressed the phone to my ear. "This is Anna."

"What time will you be home, baby?" It was Earl Grey!

"Why did you call my boss's phone?" I asked, as my supervisor stood idly by with her arms crossed.

"I tried calling your phone first, but it went to voicemail," Earl said.

"Sorry, the battery died and I left my charger at home."

"It's okay. I just bought AT&T, Verizon, and every single other American cell phone carrier until I found your supervisor's cell phone number in their records."

"It would have been easier to pull it out of her personnel file," I said, lowering my voice to a whisper. "After all, you do own the company..."

"Hindsight is twenty-twenty," he said. "So what time can I pick you up?"

"I don't know yet. My shift is scheduled to end at midnight..."

"By then Christmas will be over."

"I thought today was the twenty-fifth of December..."

"And December twenty-fifth is Christmas Day," Earl said. "Look, you've been working too much. I haven't seen you in two weeks..."

I sighed. I had been sleeping in a cardboard refrigerator box for the past couple of weeks—more like napping—in between twenty-hour shifts. "If things let up at all, I'll call you to have you pick me up early," I told Earl. "Otherwise, I'll see you at midnight."

There was a long pause on the other end of the line. Finally, he answered. "Fine. I love you, baby, no matter what," he said. "Laters."

"Laters," I said.

It wasn't until after I handed the phone back to my supervisor that I realized something: I had totally forgotten to get Earl Grey a Christmas present!

CHAPTER 2

"So what *do* you get the man who has everything?" I asked my co-worker and former roommate, Kathleen.

"I don't know," she said, absentmindedly dropping the *Fifty Shades of Grey* trilogy into some poor, unsuspecting box and covering the hideous thing with a packing slip. "How about a BJ?"

"A basketball jersey? I don't even think he likes basketball," I said.

"Damn," she said. "How about a blowjob, then?"

"Too vanilla."

"Then add some chocolate," she said, winking at me.

"Maybe..."

"Or maybe not," she said. "That reminds me of the time Jin turned my hoo-ha into a hot fudge sundae. I got a *painful* UTI that—"

"Do you know what TMI means?"

"Of course," she said. "Too Many Indians."

My inner guidette rolled her eyes. "Anyway, I only have a few hours before he picks me up in his helicopter," I said. "Where would I get sundae toppings—or *anything*—between now and then?"

"Um, you're at the center of the shopping *universe*. If you can buy it, it's in this warehouse," Kathleen said, motioning at the boxes piled hundreds of feet in the air around us.

I glanced down the aisle we were standing in, which seemed to go on for miles. "You aren't suggesting I...*steal*?"

Kathleen shook her head. "Is it really stealing if your husband practically owns the company?"

"I guess not," I said, convinced. Truthfully, though, I was in such a pickle I could have been convinced to rip my employer off even if Earl Grey wasn't the majority shareholder. I was desperate, and it was the only plan I had—mostly because I'm not very creative.

"You go find your Christmas gift, and I'll cover for you," Kathleen said.

I glanced around nervously. We were the last ones working on Christmas night, besides our supervisor. "You're a lifesaver, Kathleen."

"Don't mention it. If our boss comes looking for you, I'll just fake a cocaine-induced seizure," she said. "It shouldn't be too difficult, because I'm pretty high already."

"I don't know how I'll ever repay you."

"A rolled-up twenty would be nice."

I dug in my jeans pocket and didn't find any cash, but I did find a short coke straw.

Kathleen snatched it out of my hand. "That will do for now. Good luck!"

I ditched my orange safety vest and vowed to myself that I would find something for Earl Grey, something to prove I hadn't forgotten that it was Christmas Day...

CHAPTER 3

A half hour aimlessly wandering the warehouse and I was no closer to finding a gift than I was to finding the meaning of life. I passed boxes of flat-screen TVs, Kindles, Blu-Ray players, and countless other electronic gadgets before stopping at a stack of boxes wrapped in clear plastic, the UGG logos visible. Maybe a pair of UGG boots for *myself*, but definitely not for Earl Grey. He had recently started wearing those shoes and socks with toes, and I didn't think he would be impressed by a pair of boots that didn't treat each one of his toes with the proper respect. Pass.

Next to the boots sat hundreds of boxes of Movado watches, stacked a hundred feet into the air. Earl Grey didn't wear watches. If he wanted to know the time, he would pay someone else to wear a watch and ask that person the time. Pass.

I wandered some more and found an entire aisle filled with hundreds of thousands of copies of Nickelback's greatest hits CD. His favorite band! I had never seen a copy of this album in Earl Grey's collection, so...could it be? The perfect gift?! When I picked one of the CDs up and looked at it, however, I saw that it only contained two songs (the total number of actual hits Nickelback had). Pass.

Finally, I stopped at an intersection that split left and right. The aisles of merchandise stretched for miles in either direction. I turned right. *As long as you have your phone with you, you won't get lost,* my inner guidette said. *Just don't use Apple Maps.* Suddenly, I froze: I remembered that my phone was dead. I turned around, but couldn't tell which aisle I had come down. I had turned right, hadn't I? Or left? I was officially lost. My main objective quickly turned from finding the perfect gift for Earl Grey to finding my way back to the exit.

I tried to retrace my steps. My pace quickened as I frantically searched for a signpost that would guide me back to my starting point. It was the first time in my life I wished to see a stack of Nickelback CDs. My only hope now was to camp out and wait for someone from third shift to show up and rescue me. They didn't start until eleven, which meant another hour on my own in the vast depths of the warehouse's bowels. All I had on were my jeans and a T-shirt; I had no way of knowing how cold it would get before

I was found. I needed to stay warm, which meant finding something to burn. I looked around and found the perfect firewood: box upon box of the appropriately-named Kindle Fire. I ripped a half dozen of them out of their cardboard coffins and piled them on the floor. Now to set them on fire...

If only you smoked, you would have a lighter! my inner guidette said. *I keep telling you to start.*

"Shove it," I told her. "I'm not going to start smoking just on the off-chance I need a lighter."

It could save your life.

"It could kill me," I said. "And if you don't shut up, I'm going to kill *you*."

Oh my...

"That's it," I said, preparing to fight my inner guidette to the death. Then I realized she was only a figment of my imagination, and I was going to have a difficult time killing her without hurting me. How did Ed Norton do it in *Fight Club*?

Suddenly, I was distracted by a shuffling noise in the next aisle. Footsteps! I was saved! Or was I? Who knows what horrors stalk the Amazonian wilds at night? I picked up one of the Kindle Fires, sure that I could use it as a shield in case I was attacked by some creature of the night. I peered around the corner and into the adjacent aisle, and saw two short men loading boxes onto a golf cart. They were dressed in rags and sported war paint on their faces.

I must have gasped, because they turned around and looked directly at me.

"Are you...elves?" I asked.

"Are we *elves*?" one of them said in a thick Bronx accent. "I'm five-and-a-half foot tall. That's a little taller than an elf."

He looked more like five-foot-two, but I wasn't going to push it. I had no idea how tall elves really were anyway.

"Where's your vest?" the other, slightly taller guy asked me. "Do you work for The Man?"

"My boss is a woman," I said.

"No, no you idiot. Do you work for *the* Man. Baldy."

"Oh," I said. "Then yes, you could say I work for the CEO. But, technically, my husband is the majority shareholder, so I sort of work for him? It's complicated."

"You don't say," the one with the accent said, rubbing his chin. His hair was wild and untamed. It was then that I looked up and saw the faded white letters spray-painted on one of the steel support beams. *District 13*. That could only mean...

"I'm sorry, I need to leave," I said hurriedly. "I got lost, that's all..."

I turned around and bumped into a tall, muscular man with long gray hair. He was flanked by two more men that could only be described as savages. "If you're lost, maybe we can help," the tall man said.

But I knew immediately that they did not intend to help me. I was no longer on U.S. soil...

CHAPTER 4

Years before I started working there, a warehouse employee had stumbled upon District 13 by accident. I'd only heard bits and pieces of the story, but supposedly an entire tribe of natives was found living in a section of the warehouse the size of a football field. No one knew if the natives had been there first, or if they had moved in after the warehouse was built, but one thing was certain: they weren't to be moved. At least that's what I was told. Allegedly, the government had granted them immunity or asylum or something of that sort, and the area they were inhabiting was turned into a reservation, where they could continue to live, hunt, and farm as they had been doing for centuries. It was a fantastical story that I had never believed, at least not until I happened upon District 13 myself.

In quick order, the savages tied my hands behind

my back using nylon rope. It reminded me of the games I played with Earl Grey. Next, they blindfolded me and told me to start walking. There was just one problem. "I can't walk with my eyes closed," I protested.

"What do you mean, you can't walk with your eyes closed?" the gruff one said.

"I mean exactly what I said. I can't walk with my eyes closed."

"Maybe we should take her blindfold off," the other savage said.

"What? No way. That's ridiculous."

"What if she falls?"

"She won't *fall*, you nitwit."

"I will too," I said.

"Shut. Up. And. Start. Walking."

I tried to imagine my left foot going forward, followed by my right foot, and then...what? Repeat steps one and two. Right? It was all so confusing without being able to see my feet! I gingerly stepped my left foot forward, and wobbled ever so slightly... "I'm falling!" I shouted.

One of the savages gripped my arm to steady me and removed the blindfold. "Thank you," I said.

"I swear you are dumber than the cast of *Fox and Friends* on whippits," the New York savage said. He didn't appear to be happy that his friend had removed the blindfold. "Now *move*."

"Okay, okay," I said. The five savages flanked me on all sides so I couldn't run for it, but really, where would I run? I was as good as dead: no one could save me from the District 13 savages' villainous clutches.

CHAPTER 5

I was brought to a large makeshift building composed entirely of empty boxes. "Inside," one of the savages said, prodding me with the sharp end of his spear. I walked through the door. Sitting on a throne of printed books was a man shrouded in darkness, the only light coming from strings of Christmas lights draped from the ceiling.

"We caught her inside the perimeter, sir."

"Thank you," the man on the throne said. "Stand guard outside. I wish to speak with her in private." The savages left.

"So, we finally meet...Mrs. Earl Grey."

Dammit! He knew my name. "You can't keep me here. Earl Grey will find you!"

"And what?" the man said, still cloaked mostly in darkness. All I could make out was a tight black shirt and jeans; his face was almost entirely hidden. "Will he buy you back? Is that what you think this is, ransom?"

"I have no quarrel with you or your savages. I didn't mean to enter District 13. It was an accident."

"Or maybe it was fate."

"Fate?"

"Do you believe in fate, Miss Grey?"

"I don't know," I said. "I've never thought about it, I guess."

"How is that possible? You're, what, twenty-three? And you've never once contemplated the interconnectedness of the universe and your place within it?"

"Not once," I said. It was true: I just didn't ever think about such things. Maybe if I did, I wouldn't always get myself into such stupid situations.

"You called us savages," the man said. "But do we not resemble learned men?"

"Your 'men' wear rags and paint their faces. They carry spears. What would you call them?"

"Warriors."

"Warriors? In what? What 'war' are they fighting?"

"We are fighting for the future of publishing."

"You're just a bunch of natives," I said.

"Natives! I can assure you that my warriors are indeed native, at least to this building. They are all ex-employees, recruited to the cause." The man stepped down off his throne and walked slowly toward me. I didn't flinch. What could I do? My arms were still bound behind my back, and the door was guarded. When the man was just two feet from my face, I could make out his visage finally: the black turtleneck sweater, the thin-rimmed glasses, the scruffy facial hair...

"Elvis Presley!" I said.

"What? No, no, no. Steve Jobs."

"Who?"

"Co-founder and ex-CEO of Apple? The inventor of that iPhone you carry?"

"Doesn't ring a bell."

"I'm Steve Jobs. Ain't nobody who don't know who Steve Jobs is."

"Sorry," I said. "I like my iPhone, though."

"Damn straight you do," he said. "I still can't believe you aren't astonished to see me alive."

"See, that's why I thought you were Elvis," I tried to explain. "Most dead white guys look the same to me."

He shook his head. "I'm not dead. Just in hiding, training an army to one day retake the future of publishing—and, by extension, the *future of the world* —from Seattle's favorite son. The only way to do that is by using his own people against him. It's the ultimate inside job."

"Did you invent the iPad too?"

"What?"

"Did you invent the iPa—"

"I heard your question. Didn't you hear anything I just said? I explained my big, bad master plan to you, and you're asking if I invented the iPad?"

I nodded.

"Yes," Steve Jobs said, with a sigh. "Guards! Take Miss Grey to a holding cell."

"Wait, so that's it?" I asked as the guards surrounded me. "You're not letting me go?"

"Of course not," he said. "We'll return you—unharmed—to Earl Grey in exchange for his majority stake in Amazon."

"I thought you weren't going to hold me ransom!"

"I never said that. I did dodge the question, because I had to explain my master plan to you."

"So once you control the biggest retailer on Earth, then what?"

"Then I merge it with Apple and create the largest technology-publishing-retail corporation ever seen. I'll use my newfound market clout to squeeze the last juice out of Barnes and Noble, Penguin, and whatever other players are left in the publishing business."

"You'll destroy them all!"

"We'll have to, you see, if we want to rebuild everything in my image," he said.

"You have some kind of sick God complex. This

isn't about the 'future of publishing' at all—it's just one big ego trip for you."

Before he could respond, there was a loud crash as one side of the building toppled to the ground. There was a flurry of hooves and sleigh bells, which could only mean one thing...

"Santa Claus?" Steve Jobs said, picking himself up from a shamble of boxes and facing down the Man in the Red Suit. Santa Claus was sitting in an enormous metal sleigh, pulled by eight reindeer.

"Am I interrupting anything?" Santa said.

"Sort of," Steve Jobs said.

"I'll make this quick, then," Santa said, pulling a pair of Glock handguns from his leather belt and aiming them at Steve Jobs. "Have you been naughty or nice?"

Steve Jobs hesitated. "Nice."

"Wrong answer," Santa said, spreading his arms wide and firing the guns five times in quick succession, putting a bullet through the head of each of Jobs' henchmen. "Now I'm going to ask you again: Have you been naughty, or have you been nice?"

"If you put it that way, I guess I've been naughty, Santa," Steve Jobs said. "Very, very naughty." With superhuman speed, he pulled a ninja throwing star from his jeans pocket and flung it at Santa, knocking both guns to the ground with a ricochet shot. Before Santa could retrieve his weapons, Steve Jobs launched himself at me and tackled me to the ground. When he stood me back up, he had a curved dagger to my throat. Santa pointed the guns back at him. "Take the shot," I said. "Take the shot!"

"You trust Santa with your life, little girl?" Steve Jobs said. I could smell the Dr. Pepper on his breath. "Drop the guns."

Santa set the guns down.

"Now raise your hands, Kris Kringle," Steve Jobs said. "Nice and slow."

Santa raised his gloved hands into the air. "Just let the girl go," he said.

"I'm afraid I can't do that," Steve Jobs said, holding the blade firm against my throat. My hands were still tied; I was useless. Even worse, I was about to be used as a pawn in Steve Jobs' bid for world domination. Once Earl Grey showed up, he would have no choice but to bargain for my life.

"You're a dead man walking, Jobs," Santa said.

"That's what most would say, ha ha!"

Santa lowered his right hand quickly and laid a finger aside his nose. This was obviously some sort of signal, because the reindeer sprang to life, charging straight at Steve Jobs! He shoved me to the side and flung his dagger into the throat of the lead reindeer. Hot blood spewed from the wound, but the pack didn't slow. Santa snapped the reins as they trampled Steve Jobs.

I turned away, but could hear what happened next: After the deer were done tenderizing their victim, they began to bite into him with their powerful jaws and tear away chunks of flesh. The cries—of the deer, of Steve Jobs—were inhuman and gave me the chills. And then, silence. The feeding frenzy was over. Steve Jobs was finally, once and for all, dead.

CHAPTER 6

The remaining District 13 warriors were rounded up by Santa and his reindeer, and willingly surrendered once they saw the carnage Santa hath wrought. Santa tied the two dozen men and women up and left them for the police.

"You forgot one thing," I said to Santa as we stood and surveyed his handiwork.

"What's that?"

"I'm still tied up."

Santa winked at me. "Maybe that's how I like you."

"Are you hitting on me, Santa?"

He reached a hand up to his beard and pulled it down, revealing...

"Earl Grey!" I exclaimed.

"You didn't really think I was Santa, did you?"

"No, of course not," I lied.

"Are you disappointed?"

"That you're not Santa? Not really," I said. "Because Santa comes only once a year..."

"Poor guy."

"I'll say," I said. "How did you find me?"

"I had a tracking device implanted under your skin, in your upper left arm."

"When did you do that?" I asked.

"It's not important," he said. "What's important is that I was able to save you. If I hadn't found you, who knows what would have happened?"

"Well, I know—Mr. Jobs pretty much told me his entire evil plan."

"Oh. Okay, then."

"There's a small problem still," I said. "I forgot to get you a Christmas present. That's how I got myself into this whole mess. I'm sorry."

"You're all the present I need, baby," Earl Grey said.

"Really? Because Kathleen suggested I also give you a BJ."

"That sounds wonderful, actually," he said, unhooking his belt.

"Great!" I said. "I have only one question: Who's your favorite basketball player?"

AUTHOR INTERVIEW

ANDREW SHAFFER

A 2012 Q&A with Andrew Shaffer, the writer (allegedly) behind the pen name "Fanny Merkin."

Why do you think *Fifty Shades of Grey* and its two sequels have sold so well and captured the attention of so many people?

That's the half-a-billion dollar question! Every publisher and movie studio is on the lookout for the "next *Fifty Shades*" at this point. Is it the explicit sex? Is it the BDSM? Is it the series' origins as fanfic? Is it the "discreet" nature of ebooks? Is it the covers? I don't think anyone can answer that definitively. When I started writing the parody, the entire series had only sold 100,000 copies total. Now it's sold over 30 million copies in the English language.

I think the series has captured the attention of so many people for a number of reasons, not the least of which is that everybody is talking about the books. In the few rare instances when a book reaches a certain cultural tipping point, it feels like you're part of a giant book club. This happened with *The Hunger Games*, the Harry Potter books, and *Twilight* to some extent. I was reading my Kindle by the pool a few weeks ago, and a complete stranger asked me if I was reading *Fifty Shades of Grey*. "Never heard of it," I lied.

As a reviewer of romance and erotica books [for the now-defunct *RT Book Reviews* magazine], what did you think of the *Fifty Shades* series? Are they typical of the genre?

What stood out for me about *Fifty Shades of Grey* was how unpolished the writing was. The books were riddled with grammatical errors, and the repetitious words ("oh my") got under my skin. The sex was very well-written, I must say. Readers have obviously been more forgiving than I was in my assessment. They've looked past that and connected with the characters, something I couldn't do.

Another thing that stood out was that, compared to most of the romance, erotica, and women's fiction that I've read, *Fifty Shades of Grey* was a throwback to an earlier era with the rich hero and the virgin heroine. Most romance today features stronger, more sexually experienced heroines, and more down-to-earth heroes. Harlequin has one line of books, Harlequin Presents, that features old school romances in the vein of *Fifty Shades of Grey*, although they're nowhere near as explicit.

What inspired you to write a parody of *Fifty Shades of Grey*?

I had been trying to write a romance novel for a couple of years, but my attempts to do so failed pathetically. When I would read a page or two aloud to my girlfriend, erotica writer Tiffany Reisz, she would laugh. [Editor's Note: They are now married.] That wasn't the response I was going for! I was trying to write a serious book, but it sounded like a parody.

While I was reading *Fifty Shades of Grey*, I realized that the super-serious, super-rich hero who was into BDSM had the potential to be a great comic character. There were also a number of issues raised by the popularity of *Fifty Shades of Grey*, such as the ethics and legalities of fanfiction, that I thought would be fun to address in a humorous way. I sort of married those ideas with my failed attempts at writing a romance novel, and *Fifty Shames of Earl Grey* was born.

What were your research and writing processes like?

I wrote the first draft of *Fifty Shames of Earl Grey* very quickly, so I had to take a few shortcuts with my research! Instead of reading all four *Twilight* books, for instance, I watched the movies. I had also read the first two books in the *Fifty Shades of Grey* trilogy, but had to have a friend summarize the third one for me because I simply didn't have the time to read it. After *Fifty Shames of Earl Grey* sold, I worked for two months with my editor at Da Capo Press to revise it and perfect the humor.

What do you think is the biggest challenge facing the erotic novel genre today?

Sales have never been better. The *Fifty Shades of Grey* books have broken down a lot of barriers as far as where erotica is sold—Target and Walmart are carrying a couple of titles now that I doubt they would have touched in the pre-*Fifty Shades of Grey* world. Erotic romance and erotica ebooks are consistent sellers online. So that's all good news!

The one challenge I see is with the increasing proliferation of ebooks that are little more than porn. There are tens of thousands of five to twenty-five page "books" on Kindle and other ebookstores that are nothing more than *Penthouse* letters. No plot—just sex scenes. I would hate to see some of the online bookstores go after "real" erotica and erotic romance (stuff with characters and stories!) in an effort to "clean up" some of the trash that's out there.

Who would you want to play Anna Steal and Earl Grey in the movie version of your book, and who would you like to see play the protagonists in the movie version of *Fifty Shades of Grey*?

Anna Faris (*Scary Movie, The House Bunny*) is my top choice for Anna Steal. I wrote the book with the Zuckerberg spoof movies in mind—in a perfect world, Earl Grey would be played by Leslie Nielsen (*Naked Gun*). Sadly, since that's not possible, I would give the tea cup to a serious actor with some *gravitas*, like Leonardo DiCaprio. Or maybe Christian Bale. I'm sure Bale's asking price has dropped now that he won't be playing Batman any longer.

As for the *Fifty Shades of Grey* movie, if they cast anyone besides Channing Tatum and Emma Stone, the internet will have to file criminal charges against the producers [Editor's Note: Charges were not filed].

Why did you choose Seattle and Portland as the setting for your book? Aren't you from Iowa originally? Why not set the book there?

I lived in Iowa for thirty-three years, yes. I've never

been in Portland—but that didn't stop E. L. James from setting her books there, so why should it stop me from setting mine there? I've seen *Portlandia*, so I have a pretty good feel for the city. [Editor's Note: Andrew Shaffer subsequently moved to Portland in 2014, and was run out of town in short order.]

On a serious note, I love the Pacific Northwest. I've visited Seattle and it's one of my favorite cities. They've given us so much: grunge music, Ken Griffey Jr., Starbucks, Microsoft, Amazon... I thought I would "give something" back with *Fifty Shames of Earl Grey*.

Do you think *Fifty Shades of Grey* demeans women? Were you concerned about that when writing your parody?

I don't think *Fifty Shades of Grey* demeans women, although some people take that stance—Dr. Drew, for instance, called it "violence toward women." While the relationship between Christian Grey and Anastasia Steele is clearly pathological, it's also fiction. It should be taken with a grain of salt. Just because women enjoy reading about a woman submitting in the bedroom to a billionaire playboy doesn't mean that they want the sexual revolution repealed, as *Newsweek* suggested. Women understand that *Fifty Shades of Grey* a fantasy. While writing the parody, I was very conscious not to mock the women who read and enjoyed the original books.

Do you worry what people will think of you when they read the sex scenes in your book?

My grandmother recently read *Fifty Shames of Earl Grey* on her Nook. I have not spoken to her since. So I'm a little concerned! [Editor's Note: They have since reconciled.] But I'm more worried that people will wonder how many of Earl Grey's fifty shames are actually mine. Do I listen to Nickelback? No. Do I eat at Olive Garden? No. Do I shop at Walmart? Well, I used to work there, so old habits are hard to break...

Who would you most, and least, like to read your book aloud to?

I'd like to read it out loud to E. L. James, because I think she would find it funny. I mean, *Fifty Shades of Grey* is not without its humor, and she seems to be good-natured about some of the parody videos out there. [Editor's Note: Shaffer met James in 2013, and will tell you all about it if you buy him a coffee. A large coffee.]

I'd least like to read it aloud to the U.S. Supreme Court. They don't seem like a very fun audience.

FIFTY SHADES OF GOLD

AN ESSAY

ANDREW SHAFFER

This essay originally appeared in the anthology Fic: Why Fanfiction Is Taking Over the World, *edited by Anne Jamison.*

When James W. Marshall discovered gold at Sutter's Mill in Coloma, California, on January 24, 1848, he inadvertently triggered a mass influx of settlers to California that came to be known as the California Gold Rush. Similarly, when Random House signed E. L. James to a seven-figure, multi-book deal for her *Fifty Shades* series in March 2012, it was the shot heard round the publishing world. Not only was fanfiction now fair game as a farm system for the next generation of writers, but it was an oil reserve just sitting there untapped. Every agent and editor pointed their browser to *www.fanfiction.net* the day *Publishers Marketplace* announced that Random House paid seven figures for former *Twilight* fanfiction. Everyone wanted to get in on the gold rush.

By now, the story of *Fifty Shades* is familiar and tired: forty-something mother of two becomes a worldwide sensation by writing *Twilight* fanfiction under the pen name "Snowqueens Icedragon." After changing the characters' names, revising and re-structuring her work as a trilogy, she releases the books through a small Australian press. And fans can't get enough. Within a year, the press sells a combined 100,000 print and ebook copies of the *Fifty Shades* books. When a *New York Post* reporter catches wind of the racy books making the rounds of wealthy mothers in the Hamptons and publishes a subsequent expose, the books *blow up*. Not just explode:

they actually *blow the fuck up*. They top the Amazon ebook charts for weeks on end; bookstores can't keep the thirty-dollar print-on-demand editions in stock. Dr. Drew is talking about them on *The Today Show*. And then Random House buys the trilogy and re-publishes them with only minimal edits so as to get them in stores as quickly as possible. It turns out they didn't need to worry about the fever dying down: the re-released *Fifty Shades* trilogy spent an unprecedented six months on top of the *New York Times* and Amazon bestseller charts, dominating the national and international consciousness in a way no other book had.

Well, not since *Twilight* ended, that is. Which brings up a question, one that was in the minds of every publishing industry professional scouring fanfiction websites in search of the next *Fifty Shades*: Isn't there something *wrong* with this? Isn't there something wrong with co-opting a living author's work and fanbase? Of course, copycats were not a new phenomenon: blockbusters had been spawning them forever ("If you liked X, you'll love Y!"). But this was different. Random House was not publishing a vampire novel because *Twilight* had proven there was a market for paranormal romance; Random House was publishing a series that copied another book on a micro level, character by character (Edward = Christian, Bella = Anastasia, Jacob = Jose). This wasn't so much marketing a similar work to a fanbase as it was using Meyer's characters and fans as a springboard.

New York Times bestselling author Jodi Picoult was one of the few authors to speak out about the shady origins of *Fifty Shades*. "If u like [erotica], read erotica," Picoult tweeted. "But read authors who create their own characters and don't steal a fan base another author worked hard for. [James'] readers wanted more of Meyer's characters, & tuned in. If she hadn't started as fanfic would she have been as popular?" Still, she acknowledged shades of gray when dealing with the ethics of publishing fanfiction. "Interesting to ask where to draw line: is [*Pride and Prejudice and Zombies*] suspect too?" she tweeted.

I was also a vocal critic of the "pull-to-pub" trend (pulling fanfiction offline and publishing it for profit, also called "removing the serial numbers" when changing the names to avoid legal complications). In fact, I announced on Twitter that I would write fanfiction of *Fifty Shades of Grey* and put vampires back *into* the story. I started writing a parody, titled *Fifty-one Shades* (because it was "one better than *Fifty Shades of Grey*, an oblique reference to one of my favorite satirical films, *Spinal Tap*), and serialized it on my blog for free, posting a few paragraphs a day. I joked that as soon as I had a chance to "cash out" with a publisher, I would change the title and character names a la E.L. James.

After just three days, the unthinkable happened:

I received the first of several inquiries from publishers. My agent asked me how quickly I could finish the book; I said I thought I could have it completed within a week. One case of Red Bull and seven days later, I e-mailed the rough draft to my agent; a week later, I had a book deal with Da Capo Press. Da Capo rushed production to get the ebook and print editions out as quickly as possible—although I spent two months revising the manuscript with my editor, to ensure we were putting out the best book we were capable of. And, true to my word, I changed the title (to *Fifty Shames of Earl Grey*) and changed the characters' names.

Despite my jokes, it wasn't "fanfiction of fanfiction," but instead a parody that lampooned *Fifty Shades of Grey*, erotic romance, and the media's coverage of the whole affair. Still, I dropped hints throughout *Fifty Shames of Earl Grey* that the hero, Earl Grey, was secretly a vampire. In the acknowledgments, I also thanked Stephenie Meyer—who, in an ironic twist, was not thanked by E.L. James in the *Fifty Shades* books' acknowledgments. I felt like I had righted a wrong in the universe. But had I? Or was I, in fact, guilty of the same ethical infraction leveled at E.L. James—namely, profiting from another writer's creations and fanbase?

Parodies are legally protected in the United States and Canada. They serve a critical function in society, to mock and question pop culture. Fanfiction, by contrast, doesn't (at first) appear to serve any function other than to let fans get their rocks off. But isn't some fanfiction just as transformative as parody? Especially alternate universe fanfics, where the characters are changed from vampires to kinky businessmen. Had I been too swift in my judgment of *Fifty Shades of Grey*? Was E.L. James and her publishers just as entitled to their profits as I was to mine? The more I thought about the question, the more complicated it seemed to become.

For writers and artists born into the pop-culture saturated 20th and 21st centuries, fanfiction is an important stepping stone in their creative evolution. My first experience with fanfiction was in the third grade. I was a huge *Teenage Mutant Ninja Turtles* fan: I had the comic books, I played the Nintendo video game, I watched the cartoons. Hell, I even tried to learn to skateboard because that's how the Turtles rolled. I wrote and illustrated my own TMNT comics in college-ruled notebooks (college-ruled because they made me feel more grown-up than standard-ruled, even though the thin blue lines got in the way of the drawings, but whatever).

One of my teachers caught me drawing in class instead of paying attention, and, to her eternal credit, she didn't scold me. No. Instead, she asked me to contribute a monthly TMNT four-panel comic strip, to be printed in the grade-school newsletter sent to every home in the school district.

I think I only drew three "episodes," though, since we were close to the end of the school year—and, horrors!, my big debut in the comic book world thus ended on a cliffhanger. There are probably classmates still waiting for me to finish my TMNT saga.

But here's the thing: even at the time, I, a third grader, *knew* that it was somehow "wrong" to print these characters without permission. The school was letting me do it, though, so what did I care?

That was sort of the publishing industry's informal response. What did it matter if we're now in the "pull-to-pub" game? Stephenie Meyer never said a word about *Fifty Shades*. Everyone kept waiting for the other shoe to drop, for some nasty litigation now that millions of dollars were changing hands...but nothing happened. And so the publishing world descended on the fanfiction forums in a feeding frenzy...

Penguin's Berkley imprint picked up Sylvain Reynard's *Gabriel's Inferno* and *Gabriel's Rapture* in a "substantial seven-figure," two-book deal in August 2012. *Gabriel's Inferno* began life as the *Twilight* fanfiction *The University of Edward Masen*, under the pen name Sebastien Robichaud. Once the fanfictiontion picked up considerable steam, Reynard removed the completed work and published it with

Omnific Publishing in April 2011 under the new title—with the characters' names changed, of course. Reynard made the decision at the urging of his readers, he explained. "I was listening to the thousands of messages sent to me by readers who wanted the story to be published," he wrote in a blogpost that April. "So of course I didn't expect a backlash at the publication's announcement. In fact, the [negative] reaction of some, including those I called friends, has greatly surprised me." A few months later, Simon & Schuster's Gallery imprint bought the rights to Christina Hobbs and Laruen Billings' *Beautiful Bastard*, a reworking of the *Twilight* fanfiction hit *The Office.* The deal was reported, again, as "substantial"—meaning major publishers are plunking down serious money, all in the hopes of tapping into the same success that E. L. James found with *Fifty Shades.*

The "angry" fans that Reynard alluded to have voiced their displeasure with this new phenomenon on forums and in Goodreads and Amazon reviews. One anonymous reviewer, using the name "VanessaLovesBooks," left this one-star review on Amazon for Tara Sue Me's *The Submissive*, another former *Twilight* fanfic: "Save your money, this is another fanfiction story, THAT WAS FREE, in which now the author is using Stephenie Meyer's fans to sell their books." Australian blogger Bianca wrote on her blog *WriterlingWorks* about the trend, "Can't *anybody* come up with anything original anymore? Or are we just going to exhaust this thing ad nauseam just for a few extra dollars? The snake is eating itself!"

The controversy over "pull-to-publish" and "filing the serial numbers off" fanfiction has so far been limited to online fanfiction communities, and has not hurt any of the former fanfiction novels in the marketplace. The general public simply doesn't seem to care about such ethical questions. All most readers are looking for is a good story. And if that story resembles another story they liked, then all the better (which probably goes double for Hollywood executives in charge of greenlighting movies). And, while many authors such as Picoult have spoken out against the trend of publishing fanfiction for profit, the fact of the matter is that while the practice may be unethical, it's (probably) not *illegal*. It's difficult to imagine a court of law reading *Twilight* and any one of the reworked fanfics and finding any infringement—in fact, that may be one of the reasons Stephenie Meyer hasn't tried to sue James of any of her other imitators. (Only Meyer and her lawyer knows for sure.) Even if Meyer or another author takes a fanfiction author to court, it's far from certain that it would set a precedent.

All indications are that the trend will continue until the *FanFiction.net* archives are exhausted. The next gold rush has already been identified in the self-publishing wilderness, where self-published authors such as Tracey Garvis Graves and Bella Andre have signed seven-figure deals. Self-publishing, like fanfiction, is currently a lawless Wild West made possible by the Internet, the rise of e-reading devices, and a publishing industry weakened by the Great Recession. In fact, the lines between fanfiction and self-publishing are blurred, as all fanfiction is technically "self-published" without the intervention of mediators (although there are wildly different economic realities, fan dynamics, and reading behaviors governing fanfiction and books self-published for Kindle and other markets).

But what then, when the fanfiction and self-publishing wells run dry? Editors and agents may need to return to panning the slushpiles for gold, a grim prospect indeed. It's no surprise that publishers and authors have begun to circle the wagons and hunker down to protect their books. In the ultimate irony, James' French publisher sent a "warning letter" in November 2012 to publishers it felt were infringing on the copyright of *Fifty Shades of Grey* by publishing books such as *50 Ways to Play: BDSM for Nice People* and *Fifty Shades of Pleasure: A Bedside Companion*. "Some of these titles, which pick up on elements of the book, are clearly parasitical," an editorial director for James' publisher told *The Telegraph*.

James' lawyers have also busied themselves by

clamping down on everything from *Fifty Shades*-themed lingerie parties to bootleg T-shirts. Her agent, Valerie Hoskins, defended the crackdown, telling the *Mirror,* "You can't just hijack something someone else owns." I couldn't have said it better myself.

WRITING PARODY AND SATIRE

AN ESSAY

ANDREW SHAFFER

A 2016 essay on the differences between parody and satire, first published in Shelf Pleasure.

Although many people use the words "satire" and "parody" interchangeably, they are technically different art forms.

Parodies are stylistic imitations, exaggerated for humorous effect—think *Scary Movie,* a parody of *Scream,* or my *Fifty Shades of Grey* parody, *Fifty Shames of Earl Grey.* Parodies may be broader as well, parodying entire genres. One of my favorite movies, *Austin Powers,* parodies spy movies in a broad sense.

Satire, on the other hand, uses humor to ridicule or expose stupidity or injustice. Satires are often political in nature because—let's face it—there's a lot of stupidity and injustice within politics to expose. Examples of satires include George Orwell's *1984* and the Warren Beatty film *Bulworth.*

My new book, *The Day of the Donald: Trump Trumps America,* is both a parody *and* a satire. Its satirical content is obvious—one glance at the cover, and the reader can guess there will be some shots taken at either Trump or his opponents. At the same time, I've parodied the thriller genre, exaggerating genre conventions for humorous effect.

There are some pitfalls to watch for when writing parody and satire. If parody isn't exaggerated enough, it comes off as a clumsy copycat of the source material. When I'm writing a parody, I push things as far as I can...and then push them even further. The more ridiculous the better.

When writing satire, you run the risk of being too heavy-handed. Don't ever forget that satire is, first and foremost, supposed to be humorous. If it's not funny, that "message" you're trying to convey won't reach its audience—they'll feel like you're hitting them over the head with it. Make it funny, though, and they'll gladly hit themselves over the head.

THE 12 SHADES OF CHRISTMAS

A POEM

ANDREW SHAFFER

Originally written for a 2013 holiday card, which was subsequently pulled from Zazzle and Cafepress because you can't even mention Fifty Shades of Grey *without getting a trademark infringement claim from James's lawyer, apparently.*

On the 12th Shade of Christmas, my
true love gave to me...

12 Leather Floggers
11 Pleasure Beads
10 Feather Ticklers
9 Red Riding Crops
8 Bottles of Lube
7 Spanking Paddles
6 Metal Handcuffs
5 Cock Rings
4 Vibrators
3 Gray Neckties
2 Silver Balls...

...and ~~The Fifty Shades of Grey~~
~~Trilogy~~ *Herpes.*

ART GALLERY

Cover for the standalone ebook edition of "An Earl Grey Christmas." Photograph by Tiffany Reisz. Based on Alex Camlin's design for the U.S. edition of *Fifty Shames of Earl Grey* from Da Capo Press.

Unreleased movie tie-in edition of *Fifty Shames of Earl Grey*. The red spot-coloring on the tampon would have really popped off bookshelves.

Cover for *Fifty-One Shades: A Parody*, the self-published novella that evolved into *Fifty Shames of Earl Grey*.

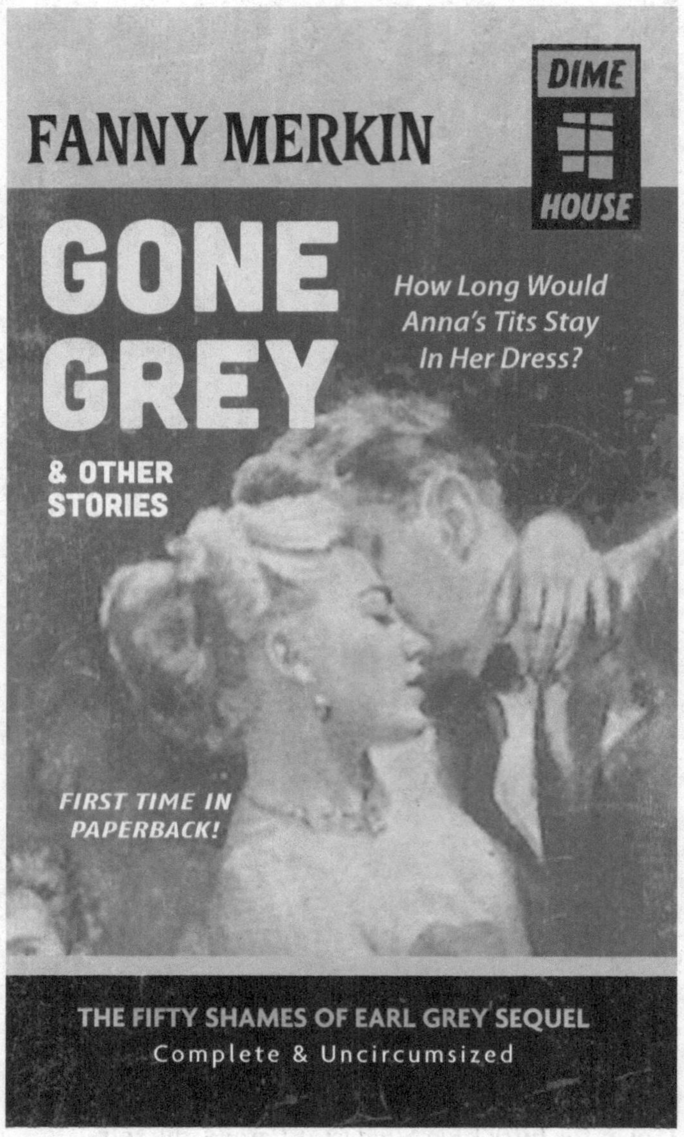

Unused pulp cover concept for *Fifty Shames Gone Grey: A Novella.*

FIFTY SHAMES OF
EARL GREY

GONE
GREY

A PARODY

FANNY MERKIN

Cover for the first edition of *Fifty Shames Gone Grey*, titled *Gone Grey: A Parody*. This cover was a play on the film tie-in edition of Gillian Flynn's *Gone Girl*.

Logo for the fictional *BDSM* role-playing game.

Facebook contest run by Da Capo Press in 2012, featuring Walmart and Olive Garden gift cards, Nickelback CDs, and signed copies of *Fifty Shames of Earl Grey*. If you missed out, bro, you missed out.

ACKNOWLEDGMENTS

Anna's diary entries in *Fifty Shames Gone Grey* are excerpted from *Fifty Shames of Earl Grey*, the full-length *Fifty Shades of Grey* parody published by Da Capo Press in North America and JR Books Ltd. in the U.K. (also available worldwide as an audiobook from Tantor Audio, as well as in translation in four different languages).

For links to buy the ebook, paperback, or audiobook, or to order a signed copy, visit andrewshaffer.com.

ABOUT THE AUTHOR

Fanny Merkin lives in a Beverly Hills mansion purchased using the embarrassingly large advance she received for *Fifty Shames of Earl Grey*.

LOOK MOM I'M A POET
(AND SO IS MY CAT)
NEW YORK TIMES BESTSELLING HUMORIST
ANDREW SHAFFER
"Always funny." — LitReactor

www.ingramcontent.com/pod-product-compliance
Lightning Source LLC
Chambersburg PA
CBHW011152190726
48288CB00010B/3290

* 9 7 8 1 9 4 9 7 6 9 3 3 3 *